The
AMAZING DAYS
of ABBY HAYES

Every Cloud Has a Silver Lining

Read all the books about me!

The AMAZING DAYS of ABBY HAYES

Every Cloud Has a Silver Lining

ANNE MAZER

AN
APPLE
PAPERBACK

SCHOLASTIC INC.
New York Toronto London Auckland Sydney
Mexico City New Delhi Hong Kong

Cover and interior illustrations
by Monica Gesue

Book design
by Dawn Adelman

ISBN 0-439-14977-0

12 11 10 9 8 7 6 5   0 1 2 3 4 5/0

Printed in the U.S.A   23

First Scholastic printing, August 2000

For Abby — of course!

The AMAZING DAYS of ABBY HAYES

Every Cloud Has a Silver Lining

How can a person be SO different from her family? I have come up with the following reasons:

1. They are aliens; I am the only normal person.

2. They are completely normal; I am the alien.

3. I was switched at birth. Some boring, ordinary family (with tangly, curly hair) wonders why they have a daughter who is so brilliant, popular, and good at sports.

4. Our family has a deep, dark secret: I was adopted.

5. What did Mom eat when she was pregnant with me?

Chapter 1

Tuesday

"He who has begun
has half done."

—Horace

Skateboarders' Calendar

Does this mean that if I start school today, I'm already halfway through the year? Yay! Hooray!

Abby opened her eyes to walls of calendars. There were big ones and small ones, glossy photographs and black-and-white drawings, calendars from many of the states and quite a few countries as well as calendars for every holiday, hobby, or interest.

Calendars greeted her every morning when she woke up and were the last thing she saw at night. The best thing about Abby's room was that she never got bored, because the calendars changed about every thirty days. Her room was like an animal that shed its skin each month to become another creature.

I have to find a World Cup Soccer calendar, Abby thought sleepily. She rolled over, turned on the light, and grabbed her notebook from the table next to her bed.

Plan for today: Do twelve sit-ups before breakfast. Run around block twenty times. (Don't stop to talk with friendly neighbors.) Eat healthy food. No donuts! No chocolate bars! Smile sweetly when Super-Sib Eva tells how she scored for her team. Nod wisely when SuperSib Isabel lectures about War of Roses. (Question: Why not War of Dandelions? Or Geraniums?) Ignore twins' fighting. Be kind to younger brother, Alex. Play chess with him when he asks. It's not his fault that he wins every game. (Be a good loser.)

Abby threw back the covers and stretched. She climbed out of bed and opened her bureau drawer. Today she was going to wear one of her favorite outfits: cargo pants and a striped tank top. She laid the clothes on the bed, then picked up a small white box that she had hidden under some T-shirts. Inside was a pair of gold hoop earrings.

Wish for today: pierced ears. How can I convince Mom to let me get them?

It was the first day of fifth grade — or, as her best friend, Jessica, put it, "the first day of the last year of elementary school." Their teacher was Ms. Kantor. She had transferred from another school in the district.

Abby picked up her journal.

Bad: I don't know who Ms. Kantor is.
Good: She doesn't know who I am. Or who my family is.

She put her journal down and walked over to her bureau. Her hairbrush lay on top of it, along with piles of seashells, rocks, and miniature plush animals. Abby pulled the brush through her tangly hair, then gazed in the mirror and sighed.

She had curly red hair that a thousand hair clips would never tame. Her eyes were gray-blue and small. Her nose — well, there was nothing to say about her nose except that it was in the middle of her face.

I have an ordinary face and extraordinary hair, Abby told herself. She would rather have had it the other way around.

She held the gold hoops to her ears and wished, for the thousandth time, that she could wear them to school. Especially today. Not only was it the beginning of the school year, but it was also the year that Abby had decided she would turn herself into a soccer star.

Abby tore off a page of her Cube of Quotes calendar.

"Every day in every way, I'm getting better and better."

Abby stared at the small, thick cube of wisdom. Why not? she thought. Why not me? I will become a top soccer player like Mia or Michelle. I will.

In the past Abby hadn't been a very good player. But now all that was going to change. Tryouts for the all-city soccer team were at the end of the week.

She stood in front of her mirror.

Think positive! Work hard! she told herself. Practice! Become a soccer star! It can happen.

She grabbed her notebook, packed it into her backpack, and went downstairs for breakfast.

"Where is everyone?" Abby asked Alex. Her brother, a second-grader, was sitting alone at the kitchen table. His hair was sticking straight up, and he had put his shirt on inside out. There was a bowl of sugary colored cereal in front of him, and he was reading a page of newspaper comics.

"You're going to turn into a comic strip if you eat that cereal," Abby warned. "Your skin will become green, and your hair will turn pink."

"Huh? Okay." Alex spooned another big bite into his mouth.

She took a box of granola from the cupboard and poured it into her favorite blue bowl. "This is healthy cereal, Alex. If you want to grow up to be a superstar like Isabel and Eva, you have to eat nutritious and wholesome foods."

Her little brother ignored her. He didn't need to grow up to be a superstar; he already was one. Probably all those pink and green food colorings had mutated his brain into its present genius state.

Abby opened the refrigerator. "Where is every-one?" she asked again.

"Eva's swimming. Isabel's upstairs reading her history book. Dad's been in his office since six A.M.," he recited.

It was only eight o'clock in the morning, and most of her family was already hard at work? What was wrong with them? Or her?

"Good morning, Alex and Abby." It was their mother, looking elegant in a navy business suit and a pale silk blouse. Her hair was gathered up in a bun, and she wore a gold necklace.

She kissed Alex on top of his head and gave Abby a quick hug.

"Mom, what's the Working Woman's Wisdom word of the day?" Abby asked.

Her mother put her briefcase on a chair. "Didn't look at it this morning, honey. I've been busy reviewing a case. Tonight I won't be home until late, but Dad will be here." She grabbed a bagel, smeared some butter onto it, and wrapped it in a napkin. "I'm late! Have to run!" She picked up her briefcase and blew Abby and Alex a kiss. "Wish me luck! I'm in court today!"

"Luck! Luck! Luck!" Abby and Alex chimed. It

was their ritual chant for their mother whenever she had to appear in court.

Their mother smiled at them one last time and disappeared out the door.

Alex's head sank downward again as he continued to read the comics.

A normal day begins in the Hayes household. Everyone is up and about at the crack of dawn except for Abby Hayes, who remains in the dream state.

"Alex and Abby!" said their father, padding into the room in pajamas and slippers. "Good morning to all!"

"Dad, you're not dressed!" Abby pointed out.

"That's one of the advantages of working at home." Her father yawned and rubbed the stubble on his chin. "Roll out of bed, grab a cup of coffee, and be at work at the computer five minutes later. And, of course, spend more time with my children," he added.

"You two have ten minutes before you have to leave for school!" He patted down Alex's hair.

"Whoa, boy! That hair is galloping off your head this morning. And let's put on your shirt one more time. You must have gotten dressed in your sleep!"

He kissed Abby. "Writing in your journal, hon?"

Of everyone in the family, Abby felt closest to her father. She wondered if she could confide in him about her soccer dreams. Maybe. Or maybe not. After all, he, too, was one of the wonderful Hayeses. He owned his own computer business, designed Web pages for his clients, and set them up on the Internet. He took care of a lot of the household chores, too. In addition, he coached Eva's lacrosse team and helped Isabel train for debates.

Her mother was a lawyer, the mother of four, a marathon runner, and she sat on the board of several community organizations.

Her brother, Alex, was a math and computer genius.

Her twin sisters, Eva and Isabel — oh, forget it!

Just thinking about what any one member of her family did made Abby feel small and insignificant. She hoped that someday she could prove that she was deserving of being a Hayes, too.

Chapter 2

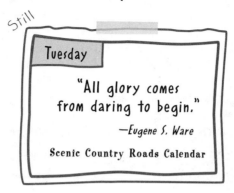

Still

Tuesday

"All glory comes from daring to begin."

—Eugene S. Ware

Scenic Country Roads Calendar

Or being forced to begin.

I wish we could just skip fifth grade and go straight to middle school.

Abby looked at her list of school supplies.

List of school supplies needed for Ms. Kantor's fifth-grade class:

Pencils boring!
Pens, blue and red Why not green and red? Or purple and orange? Brought my

favorite purple pen to school anyway.
Purple rebellion!

Crayons NO! No! I am tired of coloring. I have been coloring since age two. No more coloring with crayons — P-L-E-A-S-E!!!!

Paper, two-pocket folders, ruler, pencil sharpener ho hum, supplies as usual

A box of tissues Will we be crying?

List of supplies I wish we needed:
Rainbow pens
Souvenirs from vacation
(seashells, calendars,
rocks . . .)
Lined paper in fluorescent
colors
Favorite books
CDs and personal stereos
Earrings for all girls

"Let's go around the class and introduce ourselves," said Ms. Kantor. "Let's start with me. I'm Ms. Kantor, your fifth-grade teacher. Last year I

taught at Swiss Hill Elementary. I have two children. My hobbies are astronomy, canoeing, and speaking French."

Abby sat in the row across from Jessica. Her notebook was on her lap.

Ms. Kantor's hair is dark blond. Her nose is pointy. I can't tell if she's going to be nice or not, but so far she's okay.

"My voice may give out later today," Ms. Kantor said. "This happens every year during the first week of school. I have to get used to talking in class!" She cleared her throat.

Ms. Kantor is wearing a "teacher's dress." One of those long, flowy things. My mother looks better in her suits. She also never looks tired or flushed, and she never clears her throat. Maybe it's easier to spend all day with criminals than with kids. That's what my mother said after the school open house last year. What did she mean? I pointed out that probably some of these kids would grow up to be criminals. Ha-ha. I wonder who?

Ms. Kantor cleared her throat again. Abby hoped that she wouldn't do this all year long. One week was going to be bad enough.

"Who's next? Say your name and tell us something about yourself."

Brianna stood up. Her toenails were painted glittery orange. She was wearing bell-bottoms and a velour T-shirt. "I'm Brianna," she announced, tossing her hair like an actress on a soap opera. "I love horseback riding, soccer, and dancing."

Brianna Brag Ratio: One brag to two sentences. (Usual Brianna Brag Ratio: Twenty brags to one sentence.)

"Yay, Brianna," Bethany said, then stood up. "I'm Bethany, Brianna's best friend." She sat down again.

"Can you tell us a little more about yourself, Bethany?" Ms. Kantor asked.

"I like to ice-skate, and I have a hamster," Bethany

said, pulling at her earrings. They were tiny silver skates that dangled from her ears like charms.

Bethany is Brianna's personal cheerleader. She dresses like Brianna, looks like Brianna (except hair is blond, not dark), and acts like Brianna. Who says that science has not yet cloned a human being? They haven't met Brianna and Bethany!

Zach and Tyler stood up at the same time. "We like electronic games and computers," they chanted in unison.

"They're cute," Brianna whispered loudly to Bethany.

"No Game Boys in school," Ms. Kantor warned, pointing to Zach's backpack.

No Game Boys in school???!!! Z and T are going to be miserable. Last year they brought their games every day to play at recess and after school. If they have to leave them at home, they will wither and sicken.

P.S. Did I hear Brianna say that Z and T are cute? Ugh!!! What is so cute about them? They are loud, dumb, and obsessed with technology!

The other students introduced themselves in turn. Meghan and Rachel had gone away to sleep away camp. Jon had played basketball and visited Norway with his family.

There was a new girl in the class. Her family had moved to town just a few weeks ago. Her name was Natalie. She was small and thin, with short dark hair. "I like to read," she said in a quiet voice. "My favorite books are the Harry Potter books. I've read them each nine times. I also have a chemistry set. I like to do experiments."

As she sat down, she caught Abby's eye and smiled quickly, then looked away.

New girl seems nice. Not loud and bragging like Brianna and Bethany. Maybe she wants to eat lunch with Jessica and me. Wonder if she has good dessert to trade? Note to self:

Must stop thinking about desserts! This is not the way to become a soccer star!

It was Jessica's turn. For the first day of school she had worn overalls and a black tank top. She had pinned peace signs and little hearts all over the overall straps. Her hair was in a ponytail.

She pulled out a photo of a spaceship. "This is what I want to do when I get older," she said. "I plan to be an astronaut. I also have asthma, love apricot jam, and Abby is my best friend."

"Very nice, Jessica," Ms. Kantor said. "Next?"

Abby jumped to her feet. "I'm Abby!" Suddenly she couldn't think of a thing to say. That she had a calendar collection? Too weird. That she wanted to be a star soccer player? Not yet. That she had three SuperSibs? The less said about them the better. Who was she, anyway?

"Um, my best friend is um, Jessica. . . . Um, this year my parents are, um, letting me, um, bike to the store by myself. . . . I love to write!" she finished in a burst of inspiration.

Ms. Kantor cleared her throat. "All right, thank you, Abby. I'm looking forward to getting to know you all very well. Now let's go over the classroom rules." She wrote on the blackboard:

Raise your hand to talk.
Respect others.
No hitting.
No bad language.
Turn in homework every morning. If you forget to bring it in, you must make it up at recess.

Abby exchanged glances with Jessica. Same rules since kindergarten! Except for the one about homework. She wanted new ones. She picked up her journal.

<u>Abby's Superior Classroom Rules</u>
Stand on your head to talk.
Once a week, all students speak gibberish.
No sneakers worn backward.
Pink is forbidden.
Earrings required. Or parents will be sent to principal's office!

She slid her notebook over to Jessica. Her best friend sketched a picture of Brianna upside down, with a speech balloon coming out of her mouth. It said, "Blyzzzenfloobenpolk."

The two girls began to laugh.

Ms. Kantor clapped her hands. "Pay attention, everyone!" She consulted her chart. "Abby? Jessica? Settle down, now. Fifth grade is a very important year. It prepares you for middle school, where you will have much more responsibility."

Abby and Jessica looked at each other and sighed.

"Grade school as usual," Abby muttered. Now that she was in fifth grade, she knew the routine all too well. After all, she had been in this school since kindergarten.

She wished she were eleven. She wished she were in sixth grade. She wished she were in middle school, changing classes every hour. She wished she had pierced ears like a lot of the other girls in fifth grade. She wished she were a soccer star.

"I have a very exciting thing to tell you," Ms. Kantor was saying.

Abby came out of her dream. Exciting? Fifth grade? She didn't think so.

"This year, for this class only, we are going to have a special workshop every week. A friend of mine is coming to give you —" She cleared her throat.

"— a creative writing tutorial."

Abby sat up straight in her chair. She had never had a creative writing class before.

"The teacher's name is Ms. Bunder, and she will be coming every Thursday morning."

Brianna raised her hand. "A poem of mine was published last year." She glanced over at Zach and Tyler to see if they were listening.

Abby nudged Jessica. Brianna, a poet? What did she write, rhymes about her horse?

"How nice, Brianna. Maybe you can bring it in. It's quite a coincidence, but Ms. Bunder is a published poet as well."

Ms. Bunder was a published poet! Abby could hardly wait! What would they write? Stories? Essays? Chapter books? Whatever it was, she was ready.

"Maybe fifth grade won't be so bad," she said to Jessica.

"I hope Ms. Bunder doesn't clear her throat as much as Ms. Kantor!" Jessica whispered back.

Abby didn't care if Ms. Bunder cleared her throat one hundred times a minute. Writing was Abby's favorite subject — and they were going to have a class every week. Thursday was only two days away!

Chapter 3

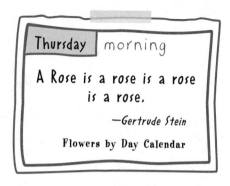

Thursday | morning

A Rose is a rose is a rose is a rose.

—*Gertrude Stein*

Flowers by Day Calendar

Roses are red,
Violets are blue,
My siblings are geniuses,
I wish I was, too.

        – original poetry by Abby Hayes

Roses are red,
Violets are blue,
Eva's a star athlete,
I'm gonna be one, too.

        – a poem by Abigail Hayes

Roses are red,
Violets are blue,
I'm sick of this poem,
You probably are, too.

– verse by A. Hayes

Who is Ms. Bunder? The eager crowd of students milling about the playground before school has nothing else on its mind. The excitement is nonstop! Some sample conversations overheard by our roving reporter:

Zach: "When you come over to my house after school, we can try out the new game."

Tyler: "I heard the graphics are great!"

The reporter moves on in search of better conversation.

Brianna (loudly, near Z and T): "The Hotshots are performing at the farmers' market on Saturday. I'm doing a solo number."

Bethany: "Yay, Brianna!"

Okay, let's try again. The roving reporter eavesdrops on another conversation.

Natalie: "Mumble, mumble . . .
Harry Potter . . . mumble, mumble."
   Jessica: "When I'm an astronaut . . ."
   What is wrong with today's fifth-
graders? They are not dying with
curiosity about Ms. Bunder's creative
writing class! Ms. Bunder's name is
not on all their lips! They are acting as
though it's school as usual.

9:02 A.M.:	Only one hour and fifty-eight minutes until creative writing.
9:04 A.M.:	One hour fifty-six minutes left.
9:15 A.M.:	We must do math. Distraction. Thank goodness!
9:37 A.M.:	Finished math in record time.
9:44 A.M.:	Ms. Kantor returns math sheet to me. All problems must be redone. "What is on your mind, Abby?" she said.
9:45 A.M.:	Reworking math problems.

10:05 A.M.:	Still reworking math problems.
10:14 A.M.:	Spelling books out. Distraction!
10:30 A.M.:	Finished spelling in record time.
10:35 A.M.:	Ms. Kantor returns spelling to me. All words must be rewritten.
10:42 A.M.:	Rewriting spelling words.
10:57 A.M.:	WHERE IS SHE??????????
10:58 A.M.:	Someone has walked in the classroom. But I don't think it can be Ms. Bunder. She is too young. She is too pretty. She is wearing bell-bottoms and a silky dark blue T-shirt. I love her sandals! They are black platforms. Her necklace is great, too. It is silver with blue stones. I wonder who she is? Ms. Bunder's college-age

daughter? Here to help
Ms. Bunder?

Abby slid her journal into her desk and watched the young woman put down a stack of brand-new notebooks. Then she glanced at the door for a sign of Ms. Bunder's arrival. She still wasn't here.

The young woman clapped her hands for attention. "Good morning, everyone!"

She was definitely too young to be Ms. Bunder. In fact, she didn't look much older than Eva and Isabel. Abby hoped that she wasn't a high school student who knew the amazing Hayes girls. It was bad enough having twin overachieving ninth-grade sisters, one with a straight A average and president of her class, the other a star of every sport imaginable. Did people have to expect the same from Abby?

Where was Ms. Bunder?

Jessica leaned toward Abby. "I like her outfit," she whispered.

Even Brianna, first in the fifth grade to wear colored lipgloss and paint her toenails, was eyeing her enviously.

"I'm very excited about this class!" the young

woman said. "We're going to do lots of wonderful writing together."

"Is she Ms. Bunder?" Abby said in shock. "She can't be!"

"She looks nice," Jessica said. "Whoever she is."

"Do any of you keep a journal?" Ms. Bunder asked.

Abby raised her hand.

"Great!" Ms. Bunder smiled at her. "Does anyone write poems or stories?"

Brianna's hand went up like a rocket. "I've published a poem," she said. "In my family newsletter."

Tyler raised his hand. "I've written a story about a kid who gets lost in a computer." His face reddened. "Zach helped me."

"Wonderful!" Ms. Bunder said. "I'm glad that some of you already write for pleasure. I want everyone to enjoy this class."

Abby and Jessica exchanged glances. Ms. Bunder's class seemed promising already.

"We're going to do a lot of writing this year. We'll be working on stories, poems, and articles, as well as writing in a journal every day."

She picked up a notebook. "I've brought one for

each of you. We'll start immediately."

Brianna whispered something to Bethany. Tyler looked pleased.

"I have lots of ideas to get you started!" Ms. Bunder took some chalk and wrote:

School Year Resolutions. Dare to Dream! What do you want to achieve this year?

Summer Summary. Your best and worst memories of the summer.

Tell me about yourself. Who are you? What do you look like? What do you love to do? Write about your family and friends.

Ms. Bunder paused. "These are just a few ideas to get you going. Choose one and write three paragraphs or more in your new notebook. I'll check them regularly."

She walked up and down the aisles, passing out the notebooks and exchanging a few words with each student.

"Abigail Hayes." Ms. Bunder stood in front of her, holding out a purple notebook.

Abby's name was written in purple letters on a laminated card on top of her desk. Had Ms. Bunder realized she loved purple from looking at the name card?

"Do you like to be called Abigail or Abby?" Ms. Bunder asked.

"Everyone calls me Abby. Except my grandmother."

"Grandmothers have their own rules," the teacher said. "Mine used to call me Violet, after a friend of hers. My real name is Elizabeth."

"You look way too young to be a teacher!" Abby blurted. "I bet they made you show your teaching ID when you arrived in school."

Ms. Bunder laughed. "The secretary looked like she wanted to!"

As Ms. Bunder moved on to the next student, Abby pulled out her old journal. It wasn't purple like the one Ms. Bunder had just given her; it was black-and-white and written all over. She was almost on the last page.

She raised her hand. "Ms. Bunder, can I finish my old journal before I start the new one? And can I write in purple ink?"

"Yes and yes," Ms. Bunder replied. "Double positive."

"I'm going to write about electronic games!" Tyler

announced.

Brianna had written in large pink letters: "Brianna, hotshot dancer and future captain of the soccer team." She drew a little heart over the "i" in her name.

Abby opened her old black-and-white journal.

Ms. Bunder's family lives near Ms. Kantor's, and she used to baby-sit for Ms. Kantor's son and daughter. Then she went away to college and decided to become a teacher and a writer. She has published poems and short stories and led creative writing workshops. We are the first elementary class she has ever taught!

Ms. Bunder has not cleared her throat once! She laughs at jokes.

She makes jokes!

We can use any color ink. "No invisible ink," was all she said. (Ha-ha. I wonder who would have tried that! Probably Zach or Tyler.)

"Double positive" for creative writing class and Ms. Bunder!!

Abby opened her new notebook and wrote at the top of the page,

New Improved Purple Journal.

Around her was the sound of pens scratching on paper and pages turning. In a few moments, she was so busy writing that she didn't notice it anymore.

Chapter 4

Friday

"To dream the
impossible dream . . ."

Making Moments Count Calendar

That song is from some play my mother is always talking about. She sings this stupid song all the time. It's annoying. I can't get the words out of my head.

Is soccer an impossible dream or a possible dream? I must make myself into Somebody. Otherwise I will be Nobody.

Abby's Soccer Goals

Turn myself into a great player. Soccer is one of the few sports that Eva (SuperSib, Super Athlete, and twin of Super Student Isabel) does not play.

How fast can I do it? Can I do it in six weeks?

Must train.

Eat healthy foods (no more potato chips).

Read sports section of newspaper.

Pick up tips from successful players.

START TODAY! DON'T DELAY!

(Does this mean I have to sacrifice the brownies that Alex and I made to a Greater Cause? Sigh. I packed two in my lunch. Maybe I will offer one to Jessica and one to the new girl, Natalie. A welcoming gesture.)

Other Goals for the Year:

Do math homework right away so seven-year-old genius brother, Alex, will not find it and do it in seconds.

(He's not trying to show me up; he's just bored with second-grade math! Too bad he can't do Eva and Isabel's math assignments yet. That would show them. Ha-ha.)

Get ears pierced.

Never eat lima beans again.

Something About Me:

I love calendars. (I have seventy-three.) My favorites are:

- an "Abby's World" calendar that my father made on his computer. It features pictures of me as a sunflower, in a stroller, and dumping pots of water on Jessica at age five.
- a Spuds calendar
- the Calendar Lover's calendar that I made, using my father's digital camera. I took pictures of my walls as they changed every month and made a calendar from them! Ha-ha! I bet no one else ever thought of doing that!

I think I am going to love creative writing class! I'm glad Ms. Bunder's name is Elizabeth, not Violet. I'm glad I'm called Abby, not Abigail. Abigail is too old-fashioned. It sounds like someone who lived during the Revolutionary War and sat in her parlor sewing all day. I hate sewing! Thank goodness I live today and not then!

And thank goodness Ms. Bunder isn't a

teenager! She graduated from college, so she must be at least twenty-two. She doesn't know my SuperSisters, either. I'm the first Hayes she has met. She said she might call me "Purple Hayes" because I like purple so much. "Purple Haze" is the name of a famous song from the sixties. Ms. Kantor says she remembers it.

Summer Summary

The Hayes family went to Vermont. SuperSib Eva biked up and down mountains with friends. SuperSib Isabel talked nonstop about Hundred Years' War. (Known to fifth-grade sister as Hundred Years' Bore.) SuperSib Alex designed computerized robots without computer. Mother read legal briefs and visited antique stores and historic towns. Father drove car, made bad jokes, and introduced self to new business contacts.

Abby Hayes purchased Fences of Vermont calendar, some maple syrup candy, and salt and pepper shakers in shape of cow.

Friday evening.

After school today, we had tryouts for the all-city soccer team. Mr. Stevens, our gym teacher, will be the coach. He says no one who wants to play soccer will be excluded. Anyone can join the team if they are willing to improve.

Mr. Stevens is nice. He never yells at kids who aren't good at sports. He tries to make them feel good about what they can do.

Encouraging pat on shoulder when I passed ball to wrong person.

"Keep up the good work, Abby" when I kicked ball out-of-bounds.

"Good try!" when I missed ball completely.

Am apparently lacking in natural talent. Will have to work hard to become soccer star.

Brianna has unpleasant habit of shrieking when person misses ball or passes to wrong team.

Natalie (new girl) agrees about Brianna.

Rachel and Meghan are very good soccer players; so is Jessica, even though she has asthma. Jessica says she will definitely join all-city team. I will, too. It is my only chance for stardom.

Best friend, Jessica, has offered to help me work on soccer skills this weekend. I want to improve before practices begin at the end of next week.

Using power of mind, I will transform myself into great athlete.

(Note: Does my handwriting reveal bold determination and an unstoppable desire to succeed? Check Jessica's handwriting analysis book.)

Why does "power of mind" make me think of superhero commercials? Will I become overmuscled cartoon? Probably not. Arms too skinny.

Went home and ate plate of cookies to celebrate decision to turn self into great athlete.

Chapter 5

Saturday

"What we learn to do,
we learn by doing."

Rhode Island Cats Calendar

What if we don't learn anything from doing? What then? *Huh?*

Bought World Cup Soccer Calendar with weekly allowance. Put it on wall across from bed. Will see soccer players first thing in morning when I open my eyes.

Read sports page today, searching for gems of wisdom. Learned that some professional athletes train eight hours a day or more!!!! This inspires me to practice without cease.

Abby kicked the soccer ball up the porch stairs for the one hundred and twenty-third time. It smacked against the door, widening the hole in the screen. It had been a tiny hole when she began her practice. Now it was not so tiny.

Abby hoped no one would notice.

The ball dribbled down the stairs and into the bushes. Abby sighed. She had crawled into the bushes many times already. There were scratches on her arms and legs to prove it.

She sat down on the steps and rubbed her foot. It was sore. She wondered if she was kicking the wrong way. Maybe soccer cleats would help.

Jessica was coming over soon to practice with her. She had promised to show her juggling, heading, and passing.

It sounded mysterious and difficult. Abby hoped it was more fun than kicking a ball up and down the stairs.

She picked up her journal.

Must keep up positive attitude. Or all is lost.

The early bird gets the worm.

I do *not* eat worms! Even fried ones.
Also dislike getting up early.

Try another slogan.

The little acorn grows into a
mighty oak.

I will be like the acorn.
Future greatness now unseen.

But what if someone kicks
me onto a concrete sidewalk? Or if a squirrel
eats me? Or if I never fall off the tree?

The little rip in the screen door grows
into a mighty tear. Will family accept this
as excuse?

"Hey, Abby!" It was Jessica. She was wearing soccer cleats and shin guards and a new yellow jersey.
Her inhaler was stuck in the right pocket of her
shorts. She was dribbling her soccer ball. "What are
you writing?"

Abby put down her notebook. "Inspiration from
my mother's Working Woman's Wisdom word of the
day."

Jessica raised an eyebrow. She and Abby were always reading, but Jessica read science fiction and fan-

tasy, not her mother's daily calendars. Abby guessed she might be the only girl in fifth grade who read calendars in her spare time. She hoped that was nothing to worry about. She already had plenty of things to worry about — like her wild, tangly red hair, her brilliant and athletic family, and the soccer team.

"Ready to practice?" Jessica asked.

"Sure. Why not?"

Jessica kicked the ball to Abby. It whirled through the grass and landed in front of her.

Abby stared at the ball. What was she supposed to do now? Dribble it? The word made her think of babies drooling. She imagined someone teething on a giant soccer ball at the end of a pacifier.

"Now pass it back to me!"

The ball flew through the air. Jessica kicked it with her knee. "That's called juggling," she said. "The ball doesn't touch the ground. You can hit it with your knees or chest or head."

"What if you played with oranges?" Abby asked. "Like real juggling? If the orange was overripe . . . squish! Orange juice!"

Abby thought of Brianna with orange pulp dripping down her face. It was a good thought, even more inspiring than the one about little acorns. She would try to remember it when Brianna was screaming at someone on the field.

"Kick it, Abby!" Jessica yelled. "Get it into the goal! That's it! Keep moving!"

Abby abruptly stopped in midkick. Three people had come into the yard: her seven-year-old brother, Alex, and her twin fourteen-year-old sisters, Isabel and Eva. They were all staring at her. She hoped they hadn't been there long — especially the twins.

Alex gazed admiringly at Abby. He loved whatever she did, no matter what it was, even if he could do it better.

Alex wasn't an athlete, but he knew every strategy for every computer or electronic game invented. Abby thought of him as her secret weapon. Someday, when Tyler and Zach were just too much to bear, she was going to introduce them to her little, skinny, second-grade brother. He would beat them at any game they could name.

"Soccer?" Eva asked. She had a firm chin, firm, well-defined muscles, and a firm belief in her own excellence. She excelled in basketball, skiing, swimming, rowing, softball, and lacrosse. Even though she was only in ninth grade, she had already been encouraged by professional scouts.

Eva wore tailored shorts and a clean, ironed T-shirt. Her dark hair was pulled back into a bun. She wore no makeup or jewelry.

In contrast, her twin, Isabel, wore her hair loose and flowing. Her fingernails were painted blue. She wore gauzy shirts, long velvet skirts, and metal chokers. No one would ever mistake her for Eva!

Isabel was the top student in her grade and loved by all teachers. When she walked into a room, everyone stared at her. She had presence, charisma, and brains. She hated sports as much as Eva loved them and was constantly arguing with her twin about the value of brain versus brawn.

Isabel and Eva were rival powers in the Hayes family. They were equal and very separate. Someday one or both of them would rule the universe — but there'd be a huge battle to divide it up first.

"Sports!" Isabel exclaimed scornfully, firing the first round in the latest skirmish. "A bunch of sweaty people chasing a little ball and getting excited about it."

"Oh, yeah?" Eva shot back. "At least I'm not flabby and cross-eyed and permanently glued to the computer."

"Better than being a mindless muscle machine!" Isabel snapped.

Abby rolled her eyes at Jessica. "Here they go again," she mouthed.

In the heat of the battle, Isabel liked to say outrageous things to get her twin angry. Eva wasn't much better.

"Ridiculous!" Eva said. "Don't listen to her, Abby. Are you going to join the soccer team? It would be great for you."

Abby hesitated. She didn't want to be used as a missile in the ongoing War of the SuperSisters. She especially didn't want to tell them what she was doing.

One day she would stun them, impress them, and awe them with her soccer talents. But not yet. They would see her at the height of her glory, not in her little acorn phase. Once the power of her mind kicked in, they'd never laugh at her again.

"I'm not going out for the team!" Abby lied. "I'm only helping out Jessica."

She smiled widely. "Right, Jessica?"

Jessica looked down at the ground and didn't reply.

Abby's best friend hated lies, even little ones. But it was too late to take the words back. Abby hoped that Jessica would understand when she explained later.

"I'm going to research a science paper on the Internet," Isabel announced, dropping the argument suddenly. She gave Eva the superior smile of the straight-A student and disappeared into the house. Alex scampered after her.

"I've got an hour before my practice," Eva said. She was golden brown from her summer bike trip in Vermont. "I'll give you a few soccer tips, Jessica and Abby."

Abby stared at her in shock. That was the last thing she needed — bossy, perfect, know-it-all Eva pointing out all her mistakes!

It was just like her to butt in. Eva always showed up to show her up.

Eva tightened her sneaker laces, then straightened up. "What are you doing?"

"We're practicing passing," Jessica said. "Wanna play?"

Abby's jaw dropped open. If it hadn't been hinged to her face, it would have fallen off completely.

Jessica knew how Abby felt about the SuperSibs! And here she was, asking one to join the practice! Never mind that Eva had already invited herself in — how could Jessica be such a traitor as to welcome her?

"If Eva's here, you won't need me," Abby interrupted.

Jessica gave her a dirty look. Abby glared back at her.

"Here, Eva!" Her best friend dribbled the ball to her older sister.

How insensitive could she get?

"Watch out! Your guard is on your tail!" Eva cried.

Jessica ran, kicking the ball.

"Come on, Abby, show a little initiative!" Eva called in a loud, bossy voice. "Get the ball away from her!"

Abby ignored her sister. She headed in the opposite direction.

Eva frowned. "What's her problem?" she asked Jessica.

"Who knows!" Jessica said.

"I don't get it." Eva stared at Abby for a moment, then shrugged. "I guess we can't play today. Sorry, Jessica. Another time, maybe." She went into the house.

Jessica caught up with Abby. "You shouldn't have lied!" she said furiously. "See what happened because of it?"

Her best friend rarely lost her temper. Jessica was calm and cool in almost every situation. Her room was neat and so was her mind.

"Why did you invite her to play?" Abby cried. "You know how obnoxious Eva is about sports!"

The two girls glared at each other.

Without another word, Abby turned and stomped up the back stairs. She didn't need her SuperSis Eva butting into her life — or her best friend, Jessica, either!

She'd work out her own training program.

Chapter 6

Sunday

"Effort is like the rain
that waters our gardens."

—Mega-Muscles

Daily Inspiration Calendar

Huh? Do I need rain? No! It would make the ground soggy and I'd slip around in the mud. They don't cancel soccer practice because of rain.

For breakfast this morning, got out Eva's *Recipes for Success on the Field* cookbook and made health shake with brewer's yeast, protein powder, tofu, lecithin, and raw peanuts.
UGH!!
Meditated to improve soccer performance. Sickening taste in mouth prevented concentration.

Jogged three times around block by self.

Ate two ice cream sandwiches to get rid of health shake aftertaste.

Kicked soccer ball up porch steps. Fifty-one kicks. Hole in screen door a little bigger. (No one has noticed yet.)

Practiced passing, dribbling, heading with Alex. Boy genius very sympathetic to my problems. He tried to coach me but doesn't know much about noncomputer-generated soccer.

Managed to conceal what I am doing from twin SuperSibs. SuperSister Eva went to swim at the high school pool. SuperSister Isabel made an emergency shopping trip to the mall for nail polish. She is obsessed by fingernails. Maybe they're her good luck charm.

Nothing will stop Abby Hayes!!!

Later on Sunday

Went to park after lunch. New girl, Natalie, was sitting under a tree reading Harry Potter book. (Question: Does she

shower with Harry Potter book?)
Told me that her parents made
her go to the park. Reason:
She needs exercise and fresh
air. She sneaked book out
under her sweatshirt.

Asked her if she would like
to practice soccer with me. She said yes,
this way she wouldn't lie to her parents
when they asked her if she got some
exercise.

We kicked the ball around for a while. I
am better at soccer than Natalie. She is
not crazy about sports. Says she
prefers to read, solve mysteries,
and do chemistry experiments. Once
she made a powder in her chemistry lab that turned her hands
blue for a week. I said that
maybe I should get some for Isabel. Then
her hands would match her fingernails!

I asked Natalie how she liked our
school. She said it is much better than her
old school. At her old school, there were
thirty-five kids in each class instead of

twenty-two. They only had music once a week instead of twice a week, and they didn't have creative writing! She likes Ms. Bunder, too.

Before we went home, Natalie said she was glad her parents made her go to the park.

Definitely like Natalie. She could be new friend.

Hayes Family News
Heard at Dinner Table

At Sunday night dinner, the Hayes family shared their news for the week.

Olivia Hayes has received a promotion to full partner in her law firm.

Paul Hayes has landed a new and important account.

Between large forkfuls of mashed potatoes, Eva Hayes mentioned that she broke the school record for freestyle swimming. She has also been elected captain of her basketball and lacrosse teams.

Her high school teachers have nominated Isabel Hayes (Lady of the Perfect Fingernails) to represent our city in a nationwide History Contest. She will go to Washington, D.C., in the spring.

Alex Hayes is designing his own computer game, which he plans to market and sell on the Web. He will probably be a millionaire by the time he's nine.

As for Abby Hayes, she had nothing to say.

Must become top soccer player. Must, must, must!

Studied Sunday sports page after dinner. Inspiring story of athlete who overcame cancer to win race. I have so much less to overcome. Must not give up. Must redouble my efforts. Note: Why don't people say "retriple" efforts? That is more like it. I must retriple my efforts.

More health shakes!

More sit-ups!

More soccer practices!

Soccer Tip of the Day: Practice using

both feet, so you can kick the ball no matter what angle it comes at you from.

  If fight with best friend continues, will have lunch with Natalie tomorrow in school. Wonder if Natalie can concoct a sports powder in her chemistry lab that will make me a soccer star. Wonder if she can make a friendship powder to reunite fighting friends.
  This is the last thing I'll write for to-day! Promise!
Really, I mean it. Help! I can't stop writing. I can't stop . . . Can't stop. . . . I am haunted by the Spirit of the Pen.
Bye for now!!!!

Chapter 7

Push-ups: twelve. Sit-ups: nine. Collapsed sneezing on floor because of dust in carpet. It's Isabel's week to vacuum. She doesn't do *everything* perfectly!

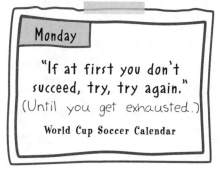

Made power shake of protein powder, dried fruits, milk powder, protein enzymes, pineapple juice, vitamin C drink, lecithin, and raisins.

Forced self to drink almost all of it. Poured rest down sink. Foamed going down the drain. Is this cause for alarm or sign that it is already working?

Read sports page. Woman who was ranked last in marathon became first through hard work, determination, and belief in herself. This could happen to me.

Jogged around block five times with back-pack for weight training. Schoolbooks squished lunch. Strawberry jelly on home-work. Wiped it off. Made new sandwich. Used powerful self-discipline and did not lick jelly from fingers.

Joke of the day: Why do soccer players never get hot?

Answer: Because of all their fans.

Good news of the day!

Jessica came over before school and apologized. She said she invited Eva to play soccer because she was mad at me for lying. She said she was sorry she had done it.

I apologized for quitting the game. I said that next time I had to fib to my sisters, I wouldn't use her as an excuse.

"Why can't you tell them the truth?" she asked.

"I try to, but sometimes I can't! How would you feel if you had twin sisters who were better than you at EVERY-THING? And they let you know it!"

Jessica thought about it. "It would drive me crazy," she finally said.

She has no siblings (lucky!) and only one parent, who is definitely not perfect!

Then we both apologized and cried and hugged and promised never to fight again. Hooray! It is wonderful to have a best friend!

I told her about meeting Natalie in the park and said that maybe we could all get together after school. She thought that was a good idea.

"Ssst!" Abby pointed to Tyler's open knapsack and the Game Boy that was peeking out of it. She remembered that Ms. Kantor had announced that she would "confiscate all games and game stations" if she found them in school.

Tyler looked at her blankly.

"Your Game Boy!" Abby said.

"Huh?"

"Oh, forget it," Abby muttered. Why was she being so nice to Tyler, anyway? Last week in gym class he had called her "fumble foot."

Brianna had laughed loudly. Abby hoped it was because she thought Tyler was cute, not because she agreed with him.

"Put away your science projects, class." Ms. Kantor cleared her throat. "Get ready for the timed math quiz."

Several students groaned.

Ms. Kantor cleared her throat again. "I know this is everyone's least favorite activity, but it will help you at the end of the year. Clear your desks and sit quietly until everyone is ready."

Brianna sat with her hands neatly folded, a smug expression on her face.

Behind her, in an identical posture, sat Bethany.

 I wonder if Bethany takes Brianna lessons. I wonder if Tyler and Zach were born with miniature Game Boys in their hands.

Ms. Kantor began to pass out the quizzes. "Do each problem as quickly as you can. If you get stuck, go on to the next. If you have time, you can go back to it."

"Ms. Kantor! Ms. Kantor!" Brianna waved her hand. "I practiced timed tests this summer with Bethany."

"Yes, we did, Ms. Kantor," Bethany agreed.

—Brianna Brag Index: Number of times Brianna has bragged so far in class: 9 (Wait until end of day. This number may be in thousands.)

—Number of times Tyler and Zach have used the word "game" in a sentence: 1,000,000,000.

—Number of times I have written in my notebook since seven A.M.: 4

"Abby Hayes, I'm glad that you love writing so much," Ms. Kantor said. "When Ms. Bunder comes, she will be very impressed with all your writing. Now put the notebook away. We're going to begin our math quiz."

Abby slipped the notebook and her purple pen

into her desk. "Math," she muttered to herself. "Math, math, math . . ."

"We have fifteen minutes for twenty problems," Ms. Kantor announced. "I'm setting the timer now!"

Abby raced through the rows of long division and multiplication. She was a race car. She was a racehorse. She was a sprinting runner. She was . . . she was . . .

She was stuck.

What was 56.8 divided by .73, anyway? Or 85.1 times 9.13?

Math was not her best subject. It was Alex's best subject. It was Isabel's best subject (though every subject was Isabel's best).

Brianna was done already! She flounced up to Ms. Kantor to give her the completed quiz.

Then Natalie was done. Before Bethany, ha-ha-ha, Abby thought as she added a row of numbers.

Tyler and Zach were done. And Jessica, Bethany, Rachel, Meghan, Jon, Mason, Collin . . .

"Time's up!"

Abby scrawled the answer to the problem she was working on. There. She had gotten most of them finished. All but five, anyway.

"A little more focus, Abby, and you'll get them all next time," Ms. Kantor said encouragingly.

Oh, great. Something else to work on. Her brain just didn't want to focus on math these days; she had too many worries.

Becoming a soccer star was getting more and more complicated.

This morning Mr. Stevens handed out permission slips for the soccer team. They had to be signed by Thursday, the day of the first practice, and returned. Players also needed shin guards and soccer shoes.

What was she to do? How could she get her parents to sign the permission slip without telling them she was going out for the team?

Her mother, the lawyer, would not sign any paper without reading it first.

Her father was less cautious but more curious. He would want all the details. Why was she going out for the team? Who else was on it? What position did she want to play?

One of the SuperSibs would surely overhear them.

It was not easy to keep any kind of secret in the Hayes family!

If she didn't tell one of her parents, she also had to figure out who would pay for soccer cleats and shin guards. And how would she explain coming home late after practice?

Abby had to keep practicing her soccer skills, too. It was hard to tell if her program was working or not. She wondered if a month was enough time to turn herself into a soccer star.

Chapter 8

Thursday

"Each step is not a means to an end, but a glorious moment to be treasured for itself."

Working Woman's Wisdom Calendar

No comment.

Number of colors of nail polish my sister Isabel owns: 35

Number of pairs of earrings Brianna owns: 18

Times per day Ms. Kantor says "Tyler and Zach! Pay attention!": 27 (average)

Times Tyler has picked his nose in class: 5

Number of lies I have told for soccer: 3

Number of goals I have scored: 0

Ms. Kantor is clearing her throat less now. Thank goodness! Today she is wearing a brown linen dress and white sneakers.

They are more comfortable than shoes, she says. She is nice, but Ms. Bunder is still my favorite teacher. I wish she would come every day of the week, even Saturday and Sunday.

Soccer Tip: Pass with the inside of your foot. Shoot on your shoelaces. The toe should be pointed.

Have trained for soccer all week. Drank disgusting concoctions (haven't thrown up yet, but gotten close); done sit-ups, push-ups, jumping jacks; and watched soccer games on television. Mia, Michelle, and Briana are awesome!

After watching, went up to room to meditate. Imagined self player like one on the Women's Soccer Cup Team. Heard the cheers! The crowd went wild. Felt the glory and the power. Opened eyes. Was still ordinary Abby Hayes. Looked at calendars for a while, then went into backyard to practice kicking soccer ball.

Alex came with me. He headed the ball

once! Said it made him feel dizzy.

Am still not a great athlete. Power of mind has not kicked in yet. Maybe it is like one of those slow-acting chemicals. One day, when I least expect it, I will wake up and find myself transformed.

Abby looked up. Ms. Bunder had come into the classroom while she was writing. She was wearing a red velour top with flared jeans. Her hair was braided into a bun with little red clips holding it in place.

Ms. Bunder is not only my favorite teacher, but she also wears the best clothes! Even Brianna and Bethany check out her outfits.

She is carrying a shoe box. I wonder what's inside it. Shoes? Maybe she is going to give Ms. Kantor a pair of platform sandals or some combat boots. Ha-ha.

"What's in that box?" Jessica asked.

Ms. Bunder smiled. "Our creative writing exercise for today."

"We're going to write about shoes?" Zach said.

Ms. Bunder put the box on his desk. "Take a look," she said.

Zach peered into the box and pulled out a strip of newspaper. "What's this?"

"Newspaper headlines," Ms. Bunder explained. "I've been collecting them for months."

" 'Giants on Rampage,' " Zach read. " 'Cardinals Stomp Opponents.' "

"Use the headlines to spark your imagination." Ms. Bunder picked up the box and gave it to Tyler. "Then write a poem or a story. You can use the headline for the title or the first line, if you wish. While you write, I'll take a look at your journals."

Abby picked a headline out of the shoe box, read it, and laughed out loud. "Snap Turns to Slog."

"That's one of my favorites, Abby," Ms. Bunder said. "I know you'll do something super with it."

Abby flushed with pleasure. "What did you get, Jessica?"

"Dressing Up and Down When Flying to the Sun." She made the thumbs-up sign. "Yes! Now I can write about outer space."

Natalie leaned forward to show Jessica and Abby her headline. " 'Chemical Reaction Overwhelms City.' Isn't that perfect? Now I can put in something about my chemistry experiments."

"Are you going to soccer practice after school?" Abby asked her.

"Only because my parents are making me." Natalie sighed and stared at her headline.

Jessica looked sympathetic. "We'll be there, too."

Natalie brightened up. "Great! That'll be fun!"

"Okay, everyone," Ms. Bunder said. "Get started!"

Abby picked up her pen.

I put the snap under my bed, and it turned to slog. My little brother stuck his hand into it and couldn't get it out. He was really mad because he couldn't play on his computer. When my sister tried to rescue him, she got stuck, too, and missed her basketball game. You should have heard the screams coming from my room!

At the end of the class, Ms. Bunder gathered up the stories and returned the journals. "Great job," she said to Abby as she handed hers back.

"Next week's assignment!" she announced.

"Write in your journals and read three newspaper articles. In three weeks, you'll turn in your own article. The subject can be anything you choose."

Jessica nudged Abby. "A newspaper article! That should be fun! What are you going to write about?"

"I don't know," Abby whispered back.

She was still basking in the glow of Ms. Bunder's "great" and "super." Those were the kind of comments she wanted to get about her soccer playing.

Problem: Still can't figure out difference between right offense and right defense. Why does everyone think it's so cool to hit the ball with their heads? Ouch!

The first soccer practice is today. I told my parents I was going home with Jessica after school today. It wasn't really a lie. At least not a big one. We are going to walk home together afterward. Maybe Natalie will join us.

A few hours later, Abby joined an excited group of fifth-grade girls in the gym. In her school backpack was a battered pair of shin guards she had taken from the bottom of Eva's closet. Jessica had loaned her a pair of cleats from last year that were too small for her but that fit Abby perfectly.

Mr. Stevens blew his whistle. "Has everyone turned in their permission slips?"

Abby stood quietly behind Jessica and Natalie. Maybe no one would notice she hadn't turned in a permission slip. If anyone asked her, she'd pretend she'd forgotten it or act as if she'd already given it in.

But what if Mr. Stevens knew that she hadn't? What if he called out her name and asked her to leave in front of everyone?

She should have confided in her father, Abby thought. He would have kept her secret. Now, if she were humiliated in front of Brianna, Bethany, and the rest of the fifth-grade girls, it would be her own fault. Maybe she would even get thrown off the team before it started. She might have already destroyed her chances to become a soccer star.

Jessica was right: Lying was wrong!

She crossed her fingers and knocked on wood. She promised that if she got away with it this time, she'd go right to her father after practice and ask him to sign the permission slip.

"Okay, everyone. We're going to play a practice game, then choose our captain," Mr. Stevens announced. "Our first game will be in two weeks. We'll play against other city teams. The champion will play for a county title."

"I'm going to be captain," Brianna announced, "of the champion team."

Bethany pumped her fist in the air.

"I admire your team spirit, Brianna," Mr. Stevens said. "Your teammates will choose a captain after our practice."

"I'll win." Brianna put her hands on her hips and surveyed the fifth-grade girls.

"We'll vote for you!" Rachel and Meghan said.

"A vote for Brianna is a vote for the best!" Beth-any cried. "Yay, Brianna!"

Jessica nudged Abby. "Nominate me," she said.

"You?"

She nodded.

"Okay." Abby was surprised. She didn't know that Jessica wanted to be captain. But one thing was for sure: If she won, she'd be a big improvement over Brianna.

The fifth-graders put on blue-and-yellow pinneys. Then they trooped outside to the soccer field to play.

Chapter 9

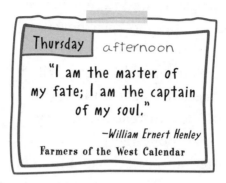

| Thursday | afternoon |

"I am the master of
my fate; I am the captain
of my soul."

—William Ernest Henley

Farmers of the West Calendar

But who will be the captain of my soccer
team? Soccer Tip: Do NOT look down. Do
NOT watch ball. Otherwise you will not
see where you're going.

"Pass the ball, Abby!" Bethany cried. "Over here!"

The ball was coming straight toward her. It seemed
to be moving in slow motion. Abby took a deep
breath and prepared to intercept it.

Now was her chance to prove herself in the very
first practice. So far, she hadn't done much to help
her side. On the other hand, she hadn't done anything awful, either.

The ball was coming closer. What should she do? Dribble it, juggle it, head it? When it came to soccer, she was like a baby who knew how to talk but not to walk.

Suddenly, as if through its own will, her foot shot out and connected solidly with the ball.

"That's it!" Jessica yelled. "Go, Abby!"

Her foot had done the job, Abby told herself in awe. A mysterious instinct had taken over. Her body had known what to do. Maybe she did have a hidden talent!

The ball zoomed past Natalie, who tried feebly to kick it.

Then Brianna ran toward it, but Rachel from the other side had already intercepted it. She kicked it straight into the goal.

"Point!" Mr. Stevens yelled.

Her teammates rushed to hug Rachel.

Brianna glared at Natalie. "That's your fault!" she hissed. Natalie shrugged and walked away.

"You'll do better next time," Abby consoled her.

She was still aglow with her success of a moment ago. Even though the other side had made the point, her pass was still a miracle, a breakthrough, an amazing moment of grace for Abby. It was a sign that she was on her way.

Mr. Stevens smiled at her. "Keep up the great work, Abby. Practice, practice, practice."

The whole world was going to love her when she became a soccer star. She imagined her family beaming at her; her teammates congratulating her; Ms. Bunder saying, "I knew you could do it." Even Brianna would have to admit that Abby was a star when she scored point after point for the team.

Mr. Stevens clapped his hands for the game to resume.

Abby ran up and down the field, chasing the ball, hoping for another chance to make a pass. But the ball didn't come her way again, or else she wasn't fast enough to intercept it.

At the end of the practice, the two sides were tied. Hot, sweaty, and tired, the girls gathered in a circle to vote for a captain.

"I nominate Brianna," Bethany cried. "She's the best! B for Brianna and best!"

"Any other nominations?" Mr. Stevens asked.

Abby jumped to her feet. "I nominate Jessica! She's fair and fun."

"Anyone else?"

No one spoke up.

"Okay, let's take a vote. Everyone for Brianna, raise your hand."

Mr. Stevens counted. "It's going to be close. Now for Jessica."

He counted again. "Brianna is the winner by five votes."

"Yay, Brianna!" yelled Bethany, jumping up and down like a cheerleader.

"Sorry," Abby said to Jessica. "You would have been a good captain."

"It's okay." Jessica shrugged. "I got more votes than I expected."

Brianna stood up. "We are going to win, win, win!" she cried. "Only the best will play on our team! Who's the best?"

"We are!" The girls roared back.

"We're number one! We're number one! We're the winning team! Only the best will play! B-E-S-T!" she spelled, as if they were all kindergartners.

Abby caught Jessica's eye.

She knew her best friend didn't care that she had lost the vote to be captain. But she still wished Jessica had won.

Not only would Jessica have been a kinder, gentler captain, but she would have helped and encouraged Abby more on her way to becoming a soccer star. Today was a great start — but it was only the beginning. There was a lot of work ahead of her, more than she ever would have believed.

Chapter 10

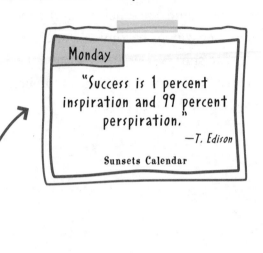

Monday

"Success is 1 percent inspiration and 99 percent perspiration."

—T. Edison

Sunsets Calendar

as quoted by my mother, who never perspires.

I am perspiring a lot! So I should be a success at soccer. Right?

I've only had one moment of inspiration! It wasn't 1 percent — more like .0001 percent.

So where do you get the inspiration? In your sleep? While arguing with siblings? With a butterfly net?

Abby's Soccer Goal Progress

Drank power health shake with protein powder, soy milk granules, brewer's yeast, energy formula, tofu, lecithin, and a few marshmallows thrown in for taste.

Double UGH!

Meditated. Did not let mind become distracted by terrible taste in mouth and sickening sensation in stomach. Focused on feet and knees. Imagined them connecting with ball again and again.

Leg lifts. Back twists. Abdominal crunches.

Reviewed World Cup game on VCR.

Practiced with Jessica. Juggled ball twice. Kicked it lots of times. Kicked self only once. Big improvement.

New friend, Natalie, joined in. She said I was getting better, too.

After our practice, decided it was time to tell my father the truth about soccer.

Number of times I cleared my throat before telling him: 12.

Number of deep breaths I took: so many that he thought I was doing yoga exercises.

Times I made him promise never, ever to

tell my SuperSisters: 16.

Kisses he got after he said, "Don't worry; your secret is safe with me. Now give me that permission slip to sign! You have to turn one in, especially with a lawyer for a mother." I gave him at least 100 kisses! And he hadn't shaved, either.

What my father said: "If anyone asks where you are, Abby, I'll say you're with Jessica. I just won't mention that you're playing soccer. You have the right to keep a harmless secret from your sisters."

Tomorrow we have another timed math quiz coming up. (GROAN) I *hate* timed math quizzes! They are hard! I hate fractions! I hate decimals! And I hate multiplying and dividing them!

In other late-breaking news, we had soccer practice after school today. I felt good turning in my permission slip to Mr. Stevens. He made me goalie for the first part of the game. You have to wear a cage on your face and layers of padding on your stomach and chest. I felt like an alien bumblebee!

The goalie is the only person in the game who can throw the ball with her hands.

Soccer Tip for Goalies
Don't try to catch the ball. Block it with your hands instead!

Brianna got really mad after the other side scored three points in a row, and demanded to put another goalie in.

If she gets this upset about a practice, what will she be like at the game?

Must rid self of habit of flinching when soccer ball comes near upper body. Try to head it instead.

The soccer game will be on television in half an hour. Must study math in meantime. Do not want to study math. Prefer to have injection of second-grade brother's brain cells instead.

Must study soccer. Must continue to watch great soccer players and then visualize self doing same moves.

Read in book that way to success is to write goals one hundred times a day. If this is what it takes, I will do it. Get ready, set, GO!

soccer goals

I will become a soccer star by the end of soccer season.
I will become a soccer star by the end of soccer season.
I will become a soccer star by the end of soccer season.
I will become a soccer star by the end of soccer season.
I will become a soccer star by the end of socc . . . . .

In this family, there are too many interruptions! Just a minute ago, Isabel barged into my room.

"Where is my nail polish?" she demanded. "Have you seen my nail polish?"

How does she have time to be a top student and president of her class and still spend every spare moment thinking about nail polish?

I held up my pale, unvarnished nails. "The evidence says I am NOT guilty."

She flew out of my room, not wasting precious seconds on apologies.

"Eva!" she shrieked. "Eva!"

If she had asked me, I would have told her not to bother. Eva doesn't care about nail polish. Alex is the guilty culprit. He is probably building a supercomputer out of microchips, old wires, and nail polish that can do all of our homework and take out the garbage, too. I wouldn't put it past him.

I will become a soccer star by the end of soccer season.

I will become a soccer star by the end of soccer season.

I will become a soccer star by the end

of soccer season.

I will . . .

This is boring! Do I have to do it all at once? Maybe I can finish later.

Need to think of newspaper article idea for Ms. Bunder's class, anyway. (Will study math in morning.)

Title of Brianna's interview with herself: "My Life As Soccer Captain"

Title of my imaginary interview with Brianna: "Bragging Brianna Bores All"

Actual title of Zach's newspaper article: "Electronic Games"

Actual title of Tyler's newspaper article: "Electronic Games"

(Wow. Exciting.)

Title of Jessica's article: "Intelligent Life in the Universe: True or False?"

Title of my article:

I don't have a single idea yet! Lucky it's not due for a while.

I will become a soccer star by the end of soccer season.

I will become a soccer star by the end of soccer season.

I will definitely and without a shadow of a doubt become a soccer star by the end . . .

Yelling outside my door. The SuperSibs are having a "friendly discussion." Sounds more like World War III. I better stop now before they burst into my . . . Uh-oh, here they come!!!

G O O D - B Y E . . .

Chapter 11

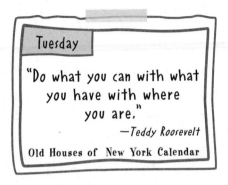

Tuesday

"Do what you can with what you have with where you are."
—*Teddy Roosevelt*
Old Houses of New York Calendar

What I did: Flunked math test.

What I have to do: Take it over.

Where I will be if my parents learn about it: Grounded.

Ms. Kantor was VERY nice! She said, "This isn't like you, Abby. I know you're trying hard. Everyone has a bad day now and then. Study some more and you can make it up tomorrow."

Felt ashamed. The truth is I didn't study this morning like I planned.

Instead stood on head to make blood

flow to brain. (It didn't work.)
Also made super power health
formula drink. Put in dried chestnut
powder, bean flour, nonfat dried
milk granules, wheat germ, protein
formula, yeast, a few soy beans,
carob powder, and some banana
chips for taste.

Do athletes *really* drink this stuff?? No
wonder they're always exercising! They have
to distract themselves from the revolting
taste!

Found five biographies of famous athletes
in Eva's room. Started first after breakfast.

Ms. Kantor almost as wonderful as Ms.
Bunder. (It's not her fault that I like
creative writing better than any other
subject.)

Will study fractions and decimals tonight
— *promise!*

Chapter 12

Thursday

"Every cloud has a silver
lining."

The Big Sky Calendar

Have you ever seen a silver lining in a
cloud? No! I haven't, either. Clouds are
white puffy things. Sometimes the sun makes
them look reddish or gold, but NEVER
silver. Who came up with this stupid
saying, anyway? It's completely false!

Passed math test — just barely. Ms. Kantor
says I need extra help. She is going to put
me in the math tutorial group.
It's true! I need help! Though not the
way she thinks.

What Should Have Happened
at the First Soccer Game

Abby Hayes made use of all the soccer tips she studied and practiced so hard. Her teamwork with Jessica and Natalie was especially brilliant. With stunning precision, the fifth-grader, who began playing soccer only a few short weeks ago, scored all of the goals in the first, second, and third periods, leading her team to victory. For once in her life, Brianna was speechless. Not a brag came out of her mouth.

"Yay, Abby!" Bethany cheered.

Mr. Stevens told Abby that she must continue drinking her power health formulas because he was going to put her in every single game for the rest of the season.

What Could Have Happened

Abby Hayes continued to improve her soccer game. While not the star player, she made some solid passes, enabling her teammates to score goals. She prevented the other team from scoring on several occasions, and even headed the ball once.

What Really Happened

I don't want to talk about it.

Aftergame Comments

"Why don't you bring a good book to the next game? And a pillow, in case you get tired. Be sure to rest if you need to." Brianna, concerned about my health.

"Nice job, Abby. Fine effort. Keep up the good work." Mr. Stevens would say this to a corpse.

"You're getting better, Abby. Don't worry; ups and downs are part of the game." Best friend, Jessica, always has something positive to say. (She had asthma attack in middle of second period and had to sit out.)

"It's just a game. I'm only here because my parents are making me. Who cares whether you're a star or not? I like you the way you are." New friend Natalie's kind words did not make me feel better.

Terrible, awful game. Missed every pass.

Let other team score winning point.

Hope gone. Cloud very dark and covering entire sky. No little beam of sunshine. Good resolutions broken. Power of mind squashed. Inspiring words useless.

Chapter 13

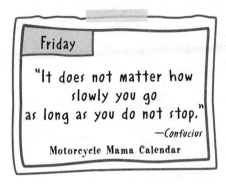

Friday

"It does not matter how slowly you go as long as you do not stop."
—Confucius

Motorcycle Mama Calendar

I read these inspiring words this morning, and they did not inspire me. They depressed me.

What if I don't want to go on and on forever at a slow pace? What if I want to spurt ahead? Or nothing?

Lay in bed this morning until Dad got me up.

Did not have heart to make power health drink. Made strawberry milk shake instead.

Recipe: two scoops strawberry ice cream, one scoop vanilla ice cream, milk, and some vanilla extract. Throw in blender and drink as fast as you can before parents or twin siblings see what you are having for breakfast. Offer some to sympathetic younger brother who promises he won't tell on you.

Returned famous athletes' biographies to Eva's room. Read comics with Alex at breakfast table.

Completed all homework.

"I wonder if Quidditch is as difficult as soccer." Natalie sighed and took a bite from a chocolate bar. "Harry Potter seems to enjoy it more."

"I'd rather be flying than fouling," Abby agreed.

"Soccer's not that bad," Jessica said. "It's even fun once you get the hang of it." She took a puff from her inhaler.

"Are you okay?" Abby was worried about Jessica. Her asthma seemed to be worse lately.

"The fall is hard," Jessica said, wheezing a little. "It's all the pollen in the air. After the first frost, things get better. I'll be all right."

"You still manage to score a lot of points in soccer," Abby said. "You do a lot better than me."

The three girls sat on a bench in the park, their

backpacks at their feet. Across from them, a group of preschoolers watched ducks swim in the pond.

"I'm not making much progress." Abby took a deep breath and spoke the words she had been thinking since last night. "Maybe I should quit soccer now before I make a complete fool of myself."

Thinking about it made her feel shaky, as if she were about to leap off a cliff without a parachute. Would she be letting her father down? Would she be letting her team down? Would she be letting herself down after all the work and effort she had put in?

Jessica came swiftly to her defense. "That's not true! You've improved a lot."

"Yes, I've scored fewer points for the other team lately."

"Someone has to help them along," Jessica joked.

Abby ran her hands through her hair. It felt even wilder and redder and more out of control than usual.

"You're more confident than you used to be," her best friend pointed out.

"I'm making more mistakes," Abby said.

"You've got way more courage and determination."

"Really?" Maybe Jessica meant that she took more

foolhardy risks, like getting in the way of the ball when it was speeding toward her. "I don't think so."

"Yes," Natalie and Jessica said in unison. "You do."

Had she really transformed herself into a confident, brave, and determined fifth-grader?

If so, it could mean only one thing: The inspiring words and slogans that Abby had pumped into her mind like multivitamins had worked.

She had built up her mental muscle to such a degree that it was only a matter of time before she became a top soccer player. If faith could move mountains, it could surely kick a few soccer balls.

"There's hope!" she cried.

Or was there?

Was she deceiving herself, thinking she could become a great soccer player?

Natalie took another bite from her chocolate bar. "I wish I wanted to be a good soccer player. All I want to do is sit in my room and read or perform experiments. My parents think I'm warped."

"Really? My parents would love you," Abby said. "They think Isabel is great, and she spends her entire life in the library. Except when she's doing her fingernails, of course."

"Wow," Natalie said. "Awesome."

Yes, Abby's family was awesome. That was the problem. She picked up her journal.

If family is awesome, then I must be, too. Genetic heritage must show up somewhere. Even if they are type A and I am type Z. Curly red hair and lack of genius are not proof that I come from different genetic line. Amazing gene must be hiding, but one day it will show up.

Right?

If A gene doesn't show up soon, will replace World Cup Soccer calendar with School Joke calendar.

Burning question of the day: What to do about soccer goals. Can I achieve them? How soon? Soon enough to make a  difference and impress my family?

Do I hope for the best and continue? Or cut my losses and quit?

Note: Why are questions burning? Can they be cold? Or soothing?

Why are losses cut? Why not sliced? Or chopped?

Must not be distracted by these deep thoughts. Back to my friends and the decision I must make.

Abby put down her pen. Her two friends were looking over their journals. Jessica had doodled pictures of aliens in the margins of hers; Natalie had written only a few paragraphs in large letters.

"I wish I loved to write as much as you, Abby." Natalie sighed. "I don't know what I'm going to do about this newspaper article."

"Neither do I," Abby admitted. "But I'll probably get an idea sooner or later." She took the piece of chocolate that Natalie held out to her. "Why don't you write a book review of the Harry Potter series?"

Natalie's face brightened. "Good idea!"

"When I get stuck writing a story, I always ask Abby for help," Jessica said.

"It's fun," Abby said. "I love to do it." She wished that soccer came as easily as writing.

"So . . . what do you think?" Jessica asked. "About soccer. Are you going to quit or not?"

"I vote for Abby to stay with it!" Natalie cried. "I think she can do it."

"You never know what you can do until you try," Jessica said, pulling out her asthma inhaler and taking another puff.

Was this a sign? Her best friend was spouting inspiring slogans just like one of Abby's calendars. Maybe it meant that Abby wasn't supposed to give up.

Jessica had asthma, but she didn't let it stop her. Abby didn't have asthma, and she was ready to quit.

Natalie was rooting for her, too. She couldn't disappoint her friends.

She hoped she wouldn't disappoint herself.

"Okay. I won't quit yet," Abby announced. "I'll stay in until the end of soccer season."

Chapter 14

Saturday

"Hope is a waking dream."
—Aristotle

Spuds Calendar

(Aristotle again. Isabel says that he lived
in ancient Greece. Wonder if he collected
calendars, too.) It's easy to hope on the
weekend when there aren't any games.
What I really hope for is an idea for that
newspaper article. It's due this week. I've
been so busy thinking about soccer that I
haven't done anything about the article at
all! I can't fail math and creative writing!
(Especially since creative writing is my best
subject.)

This morning: Made another power health

shake: vitamin-enriched brewer's yeast, non-fat yogurt, soy flakes, dried apple rings, grapefruit juice, protein powder, oat bran.

Ugh! Ugh! UGH!

Wrote "I will become a star soccer player . . ." 150 times on piece of paper. Hung it on wall next to World Soccer Cup calendar.

Exercises: Deep breathing, sit-ups, push-ups, jumping jacks, leg lifts, shoulder rolls, neck rolls, dinner rolls (ha-ha, just kidding).

Stood on head to make blood flow to brain. Power health shake flowed from stomach to mouth. Ugh!

Took biographies of great athletes out of Eva's room again and read for half an hour. Eva didn't notice.

Called Jessica and asked her to meet me in park later this afternoon for more soccer practice. Natalie is in middle of important experiment and can't come.

"Hey, Abby. What's up?" It was Eva, in

her customary outfit of basketball jersey and shorts, dribbling a basketball on the sidewalk in front of Abby.

"Trying to come up with an idea for an article. For creative writing class." Abby sighed. She had been staring at the blank paper for twenty minutes now. Her mind was crammed with soccer tips, inspiring stories about athletes who had come up from under, and flashbacks to exciting moments on the soccer field. There was no room in her brain for anything else.

Abby didn't know if Ms. Bunder would be as understanding as Ms. Kantor if she turned in her article late. Maybe she would even give Abby a failing grade!

Eva whirled and feigned a shot. Then she turned back to Abby. "You're always writing," she said. "A newspaper article should be easy for you."

"It isn't this time," Abby admitted.

"Why don't you cover one of my basketball games?"

"I don't know enough about the rules and who the players are."

"I'd fill you in," Eva offered. "You can publish it in your school newspaper, too."

"We don't have one," Abby said.

"Maybe you should start one," Eva said, wiping her forehead with the back of her hand.

"Maybe . . ." Abby echoed. It was a good idea. After soccer season was over, she'd talk to Ms. Bunder and see if Natalie and Jessica were interested.

That still left her without a subject for her article. Or did it?

She couldn't cover Eva's basketball game — there was too much to learn first. However, there was another game where she knew both the players and the rules. She had spent plenty of time observing the action. In addition, she had firsthand, personal experience. If Abby wasn't qualified to write about the Lancaster Elementary fifth-grade girls' soccer team, who was?

Hadn't she been obsessed with soccer for weeks? Here was the article idea, practically begging to be written, and she hadn't even thought of it until Eva made her suggestion.

She jumped up from the steps and hugged her sister. "Thanks, Eva. You're the greatest."

Eva smiled. Everyone always told her she was the greatest. She didn't even ask Abby why.

"You should wear your hair down more often,"

she said, looking at Abby's long curly red hair.

"You like my hair?" Abby couldn't believe it. "It's so red! It's so messy and tangly!"

"It's so gorgeous," Eva said. "If you were stuck with boring straight brown hair like me, you'd appreciate it. I've been jealous of your hair since you were a baby."

"You have?"

"Whenever you get sick of it, give it to me." Eva dropped the basketball into a bin on the porch and disappeared into the house to take a shower.

Abby stared openmouthed after her sister. This was Eva, wasn't it? Not some alien inhabiting her sister's body?

Wow. SuperSib Eva, family jock, gave me an idea for the newspaper article AND she loves my hair!!!! Stunning surprise. SuperSis can behave differently than expected. Maybe I can, too. Stay tuned for further developments.

Abby pulled a fresh sheet of paper from her notebook and began to work on her article.

Chapter 15

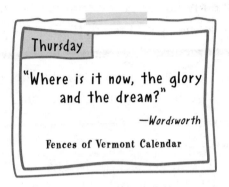

Thursday

"Where is it now, the glory
and the dream?"

—Wordsworth

Fences of Vermont Calendar

Alive, well, and kicking. It's my lucky week—and there's a game tonight.

<u>Lucky Week List</u>

#1. I completed the newspaper article and turned it in on time!

Didn't have to make embarrassing explanations or apologies to Ms. Bunder. I wouldn't want her to think I don't care about creative writing class. Because it is my FAVORITE subject in the world!

Ms. Bunder smiled when she saw the title and said she couldn't wait to read it.

#2. I got an 85 percent on a timed math quiz!!! (How did I do that? It really was luck.) .

Ms. Kantor wrote, "Keep up the good work!" and gave me a pizza certificate for my effort.

Zach said he'd rather have a computer game.

I said, "If they gave out computer games as rewards, you'd be the best student in the school."

Zach agreed. Then he said, "But no one would be better than you in writing."

Agree with Brianna for once. Zach is cute. (When not hooked up to a game machine. Then he is like an electronic zombie.)

#3. Today Brianna is not in school!!!
Bethany told us that Brianna spent last

night throwing up and is still sick today.
How many times did she puke? Could start
Brianna Barf Index instead of Brianna
Brag Index.

Mr. Stevens says that Jessica will be the
temporary captain for the soccer game
tonight. She will assign positions. Hooray!

Bethany is sulking because Jessica is
captain. She thought she should be captain
because she is best friend and best clone
of Brianna.

"It's not a look-alike contest," I told
her. "Almost half the players voted for
Jessica."

Personally, I am very happy that Bethany
will not lead our team to misery. Many of
the other players seem pleased about it,
too.

A lot of people are coming to today's
game. Ms. Kantor is coming because we are
playing Swiss Hill Elementary, her old
school. She says she will root for us and
not them.

Jessica's mother is taking off early from

work to see the game — and she doesn't even know that Jessica will be captain!

Natalie is glad that her parents can't come. They have already threatened to make her play basketball, softball, and lacrosse. If they see how bad she is, she says, they might make her take up volleyball and cross-country skiing as well.

Jessica's asthma is worse today, and she had to go to the nurse's office twice to use her inhaler. She is also nervous about the game.

She said she is worried about all the people who will be watching. Her mother isn't able to come to many of her games. Jessica wants her mother to see her at her best.

I told her, "You never know what you can do until you try," and "We must cultivate our garden."

Jessica said she didn't know what gardens had to do with it, but she was glad that I was her friend. She said she would try to enjoy the game and not worry so much about what everyone was thinking.

Have not given up hope of becoming soccer star. Sign of insanity? There is none in immediate family.

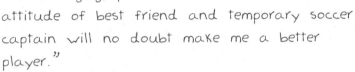

It's my lucky week. Anything can happen!

Encouraging, positive attitude of best friend and temporary soccer captain will no doubt make me a better player."

The Lancaster girls put on their shin guards and cleats and kicked the ball back and forth on the field to warm up.

The Swiss Hill team arrived.

"Okay, let's go out and have fun!" Jessica yelled.

"Brianna would never say 'fun,'" Bethany pouted. "She'd say win! Let's go out and win!!"

"If we don't win, we can still have fun!" Jessica retorted.

The team cheered. "Hooray, Lancaster Elementary!"

They ran onto the field and took up their positions. The ball went into play. Jessica passed it to

Bethany. Bethany kicked it to Rachel, who dribbled it toward the goal until a girl on the other team stole it from her.

Abby ran after the Swiss Hill girl. She came up alongside her, kicked the ball out from under her, and raced in the opposite direction for the goal.

"Abby! Abby! Abby!" shrieked her teammates.

She barely heard them as she weaved in and out of the Swiss Hill guards, keeping the ball under control. The field seemed to open up as she ran. It was as though a path were marked straight to the goal.

Ms. Kantor cheered from the bleachers, and the team went wild as Abby gave the ball a ferocious kick. It soared straight into the goal, past the goalie.

"Point to Lancaster Elementary!" the ref called.

Abby pushed her damp hair off her forehead and stared at the ball in awe. She had really done it; she had scored a point for her team.

Jessica hugged Abby. "I knew you could do it!" Her teammates gave her the thumbs-up sign as she jogged back to her position.

A Swiss Hill girl stood on the midfield line and kicked the ball to one of her teammates. The game was on again.

This was the breakthrough, Abby thought. Her moment had come. When the ball soared through the air in her direction, she headed it. It bounced toward Rachel, who passed it to Jessica. Jessica raced with it toward the goal. Another point for Lancaster Elementary!

Bethany made another point, and Meghan made another. When the period ended, Lancaster was ahead.

"I knew this would happen," Abby said to Jessica, who nodded her head in agreement.

It had finally paid off. The soccer games she had watched on television, the power health formulas she had forced herself to drink, the books she had read, the inspiring words, and most of all, the hours she had practiced were leading her toward soccer stardom.

Someday, her friends would tell the story of how she had overcome incredible odds to achieve her soccer goals. For today, Abby was going to enjoy her rapid ascent to the top.

Jessica's mother was sitting on the bleachers, still in her work clothes. She had come directly from the music library at the university where she worked.

Abby waved to her, and she waved back. She only

wished that her own family was waving proudly from the bleachers. Two brilliant moves in only a matter of minutes!

Mr. Stevens blew his whistle, and they were back on the field for the second period.

Once more Abby raced for the ball. She passed it to Meghan.

"Keep it up, Abby!" Mr. Stevens yelled. "Stay in there!"

Swiss Hill intercepted the ball. Bethany stole it from the Swiss Hill girl and passed it to Abby.

"Center! Center!" Bethany screamed. "Get it, Abby!"

Abby began to sprint toward the ball. She was just about to deliver another powerful kick that would cement her reputation as a top player when she hit a patch of muddy grass. The ball whizzed past her. She slipped, lost her balance, and flew with arms outspread, facedown into the mud.

Her teammates screamed. The Swiss Hill girls cheered. Someone kicked the ball into a goal. The ref blew his whistle and declared a point for Swiss Hill.

Mr. Stevens ran over to Abby and helped her up. "That was quite an impressive fall," he said. "Anything broken?"

"I don't think so." She was covered in mud. Her T-shirt hung from her chest. Her shin guards were soaked. Her knees were scraped, and her hands were sore.

He examined her bruises. "Maybe you better sit down. We'll clean up your hands and knees and give you an ice pack."

She stumbled over to the bench where a couple of the girls were sitting out the period. Mr. Stevens sent one of them in to replace her.

"Are you all right?" Natalie asked. "You were great just a minute ago. I was cheering for you!"

"I'm okay," Abby said, her eyes filling with tears in spite of herself. The game had started so well! Now her hands and knees were stinging, and she had the taste of mud in her mouth.

Ms. Kantor climbed down the bleachers. "Your dad and brother are here, Abby."

"My dad and brother?"

Abby turned. Alex and her father were right behind her. They had come to her game!

"When did you get here?" she stammered.

"Just before you fell," her father said. "Are you okay? That was some tumble."

"Abby! You look like a mud monster!" Alex cried.

Abby stared at them in horror. She tried to say something, but no words came out.

"Your mother wants to talk to you." Her father held out a cell phone. "I told her about your fall —"

"Mom . . ." Abby said. "Yes, I'm okay." She wasn't about to tell her mother that she had tried to prove herself worthy of the Hayes family and failed. Her pity would be worse than any scorn. She handed the phone back to her father.

"What's the matter?" he asked. "We're proud of you, Abby."

Proud? For falling on her face in front of her friends, teacher, and family? She didn't think so. Abby turned and ran.

Ignoring her bruised knee, scraped palms, and the tears running down her face, she didn't stop until she reached her house. She grabbed the key from its hiding place, unlocked the door, and went straight to the bathroom. She stripped off her wet and muddy clothes and jumped into the shower. Before anyone returned, she was in her room and under the covers.

There she stayed for the rest of the night.

Chapter 16

Friday

Nothing. No words at all, especially so-called inspiring ones. Didn't they get me into this mess in the first place?

The sun streamed into Abby's bedroom. As she did every morning, she opened her eyes to walls of calendars. There was her Cats of Rhode Island calendar, featuring an orange-striped tabby for the month of October. She gazed fondly at a photograph of mashed potatoes from her Spuds calendar, then moved over to her World Soccer Cup calendar.

Abby closed her eyes and groaned as memories of the previous day flooded back.

Her parents, twin sisters, and little brother had come to her door last night. They tried to talk to her, but she refused to speak. She lay under the covers with her hands over her ears and her eyes shut tight.

More from habit than anything else, she reached over to the night table for her journal.

Cannot face family after humilation of yesterday. Triumph unseen. Spectacular nosedive into mud witnessed by entire world. (Well, almost.)

Do not want to see anyone ever again.

Options:

Spend rest of life in bed.

Get adopted by other family in other city.

Run away and live in sewers.

Tears trickled down the side of her nose as she thought of herself clothed in ragged bell-bottom jeans and a ripped tie-dye T, hunting for rats to eat for dinner.

Perhaps my wounds are so serious I will have to spend a month in the hospital recuperating. When I come out, no one will remember me.

Abby rolled back the covers and examined her knee. It was scraped and red. There wasn't any scab. Her hands didn't have a mark on them.

She lay back on the bed and tried to look pale and sickly. "My stomach hurts," she whimpered. "My head hurts. I must have gotten mud poisoning. Call the ambulance."

Someone was running up the stairs. Abby closed her eyes and lay limp on the bed. The door opened.

"Abby! Abby! Wake up!" It was Alex. He shook her gently.

She snored a little and rolled over.

He shook her harder. "Wake up!"

If she didn't open her eyes, he'd give up eventually. She just wouldn't move until he left.

Abby lay still, pretending she was dead. Alex was here to mourn her.

So why did he keep bumping against the bed and laughing?

"Wake up, Abby!" Alex said. "You're famous!"

Infamous was probably more like it. She was a laughingstock at Lancaster Elementary and in the amazing, awesome Hayes family.

Her parents' voices floated down the hall. Now they were in her room, too. Why didn't everyone just bring their bowls and plates and eat breakfast on her bed?

"Abby, the Journal has printed your newspaper article," her father announced. "Your entire family is extremely proud of you."

"What article?" She sat bolt upright and snatched the newspaper from his outstretched hand.

"I knew she wasn't sleeping!" Alex crowed.

Abby scanned the page, then saw the headline. "It's a Kick — Or Is It? The Ups and Downs of Soccer" by Abby Hayes.

"That's the article I wrote for creative writing!" Abby cried. "I just turned it in! How did it get in the paper?"

"Ms. Bunder liked your article so much that she showed it to a friend who works at the newspaper. Last night she called to let us know that it was going into print," her mother said.

Her father beamed at her. "You're a published journalist at age ten!"

"Hooray, Abby!" Alex cheered. He jumped on the bed to hug her. Her parents kissed her.

Abby's mother checked her watch. "Oops! I have to leave in fifteen minutes. Abby, get dressed and come downstairs. Your father is making waffles to celebrate."

Abby sat at the table and gazed proudly at her newspaper article. There it was, her name in print! The Journal had written an introduction: "We are pleased to present the original and thoughtful views of Abby Hayes, a fifth-grade writing student of Ms. Elizabeth Bunder at Lancaster Elementary School."

"The original and thoughtful views," Abby said out loud. "The original and thoughtful views of Abby Hayes, fifth-grade writing student."

She took a bite of waffle, which she had smeared with strawberry jam.

Then she gazed at the article again.

It's a Kick — Or Is It?
The Ups and Downs of Soccer
by Abby Hayes

Have you ever seen a team of fifth-grade girls racing

up and down a soccer field, chasing a little white ball? It's not an unusual sight at Lancaster Elementary School, where the team meets once a week to practice soccer and once a week to play in a game against another city team. The captain is Brianna Bauer. She thinks winning is important. Mr. Stevens, the coach, talks about good sportsmanship and doing your best.

Many of the girls have already been playing soccer for several years. Their heroes are Mia Hamm, Michelle Akers and Briana Scurry. They watch the World Cup on television and practice kicking soccer balls the way most kids eat candy. Some of the girls, however, are newcomers to the game. When they see a fast-moving ball coming straight at their head, they duck and run in the opposite direction.

Is there a soccer personality? Is it an inborn talent that is developed through hard work? Or can anyone play this game? That is the question I ask myself over and over as I try to turn myself into a soccer player. I don't know whether I've done it yet. Maybe I need to practice longer and harder. Or maybe I need more natural athletic ability. I wonder if I will succeed if I really start to love the game. Or will I love the game only if I succeed at it?

I have lots of questions and not many answers. But one thing I know: I'm going to be on the soccer field this week, doing my best.

Abby folded the newspaper and took another bite of waffle. Then she reached inside her backpack and pulled out her journal.

No one in Hayes family has said a word about disastrous soccer game. Are they being polite and tactful, or have they all suffered amnesia?

I guess my secret is out now. My SuperSisters know that I'm on the team. Isabel hasn't given me her speech about "barbaric sports," and Eva hasn't told me a thousand ways I need to improve myself. Has the article interrupted their usual train of thought? I hope so!

Jessica just called. Said that anyone can fall, but few people can make a goal. Especially someone who has been playing for a short time. She said she liked my article, too. Invited me to a sleepover on Saturday night with Natalie. Jessica's mother doesn't usually let her have sleepovers, but Jessica used great powers of persuasion. Told her mother that Natalie was new in town and hadn't been invited anywhere yet.

Natalie told her parents that Jessica and I are soccer players, so they are letting her sleep over.

Hooray! That's tomorrow night!

Am thinking about soccer goals.
1. Didn't give myself enough time.
2. Did pretty well for the time I had.
3. Have become much better player — if not great one or star yet.
4. Worked hard, did best. Should be proud of effort, not results.
5. Published article in newspaper.
6. Soccer season is not over yet!

Conclusion: Maybe there is a silver lining to every cloud! (Must apologize to whoever wrote that.) If I hadn't joined the team, I wouldn't have written the article or gotten published in the newspaper.

I wonder if Ms. Kantor will put it up on the bulletin board for everyone to see.

Father told me that I will receive fifteen dollars from *Journal* for my article. Will not spend money on soccer equipment. Will buy calculator to help with math problems instead.